D1017353

# NO BEAN SPROUTS, PLEASE!

# NO BEAN SPROUTS, PLEASE!

## Constance Hiser

drawings by Carolyn Ewing

Holiday House/New York

This book is a presentation of Newfield Publications, Inc.
Newfield Publications offers book clubs for children from
preschool through high school. For further information write to:
**Newfield Publications, Inc.,** 4343 Equity Drive,
Columbus,Ohio 43228.

Published by arrangement with Holiday House.
Newfield Publications is a federally registered
trademark of Newfield Publications, Inc.
Weekly Reader is a federally registered trademark
of Weekly Reader Corporation.

1995 edition

Library of Congress Cataloging-in-Publication Data
Hiser, Constance.
No bean sprouts, please! / written by Constance Hiser ;
illustrated by Carolyn Ewing. — 1st ed.
p.   cm.
Summary: Fourth-grader James is resigned to his mother's healthy but
boring lunches until he gets a very unusual lunch box for his birthday.
ISBN 0-8234-0760-8
[1. Magic—Fiction.  2. Food—Fiction.  3. Schools—Fiction.]
I. Ewing, C. S., ill.  II. Title
PZ7.H618No    1989
[Fic]—dc19    89-1817    CIP    AC
ISBN 0-8234-0760-8

# Contents

# Contents

# NO BEAN SPROUTS, PLEASE!

# CHAPTER 1

# Happy Birthday

Every day, when it was time to get ready for school, James pleaded with his mother:

"*Please,* Mom—no bean sprouts in my lunch box!"

And every day, when it was time for lunch, James found the same food in his lunch box—bean sprouts, wheat germ, soybean sandwiches, and (yuck!) unsweetened yogurt.

"But, Mom," he begged again and again, "no one will ever trade with me at lunchtime!"

"You shouldn't *want* them to," his mother said as she dropped a bagful of raw turnip slices into his lunch box. "Your lunch is *healthy*. It's *good* for you. It will help you grow."

"Oh, yeah? Then why am I the shortest boy in the whole fourth grade?" James asked her. But day after day, his mother kept packing the same horrible lunches.

At school, James would sit in the lunchroom watching everyone else eat peanut butter and jelly sandwiches, bologna sandwiches, corn chips, cheese curls, and candy bars. He would sigh as he took a bite of raw broccoli and a nibble of bean sprouts.

But then came James's ninth birthday, when the Wonderful Lunch Box arrived.

James woke up that morning feeling hopeful and excited. Excited because he was turning nine—and that was a *much* better age than only eight. Hopeful because surely his mother wouldn't put bean sprouts in his lunch today—not on his *birthday!*

But when he pulled on his jeans and

sweater and ran into the kitchen for breakfast, his mother, as usual, was packing raw
crunchy things in clear plastic bags and
dropping them into his lunch box. James
groaned when he saw the raw cauliflower,
dried apricots, liver on whole wheat, and—
of course—the bean sprouts. But because it
was his birthday, he only sighed as he sat
down to his breakfast of wheat germ and
yogurt.

"By the way, James," said his mother, as
she pushed carrots through the juicer, "the
postman came early today. Looks like you
got three cards and a package."

James drank his carrot juice in one gulp.

"Where?" he demanded. "Show me!"

"Show me, *please,*" his mother reminded
him as she gave him his mail.

The birthday cards were from his grand-
parents, his aunt Zelda, and his best friend,
Norman. The ones from his relatives had
checks inside, and the one from Norman
had a face on the front that crossed its eyes
and stuck out its tongue when he wiggled

the card. It was a great card! But James was saving the best for last.

The minute he saw the package, stuck all over with strange stamps and stickers, James knew it was from his uncle Wesley. Uncle Wesley always remembered his birthday, and his gifts were the best of all. That was because Uncle Wesley went to far-off, mysterious places where practically no one ever went. James never knew what he might send back. Once it had been a boomerang from Australia, once a dragon kite from Japan, once even a shrunken head from darkest Africa (his mother had said it wasn't a real head, but James hoped it was).

James wasted no time ripping off the brown wrapping paper and tearing open the cardboard box inside. There were layers and layers of tissue paper, and then—and then —James could hardly believe his eyes. A lunch box. Not something strange and unusual and wonderful. Just a plain, square, red lunch box. It didn't even have a picture on it.

His mother was watching. "What's the matter, James?" she asked. "Don't you like it?"

"Oh—oh, sure," James answered. "It's fine, I guess."

Maybe there was something inside the lunch box. James unhitched the latch and lifted the lid. But the box was empty except for a note, in Uncle Wesley's handwriting, on a little white card.

"Dear James," it said. "Take good care of this. It is a *very special* lunch box. I think you'll enjoy it! Happy Birthday! Uncle Wesley."

Now James was puzzled. What was so special about a plain red lunch box? He stared at it, but it looked pretty ordinary to him.

"Well," said his mother at last, "we may as well pack your lunch in your new lunch box. Your old one was getting pretty beaten up. Hurry and finish your breakfast, James. It's almost time for your bus."

And she dropped the raw cauliflower, the dried apricots, the liver on whole wheat, and—of course—the bean sprouts into his new lunch box.

# CHAPTER 2

# Hot Dogs and Chili

On the bus ride to school, during Mrs. Saperstein's arithmetic lesson, and for the rest of the morning, James told himself that he wasn't really disappointed. Maybe Uncle Wesley just hadn't been anywhere very interesting lately. But he sighed when he picked up his lunch box at noon and headed for the lunchroom with the rest of his class.

Norman and Mike had saved him a place, the way they always did. Pete was there too, across the table, and T.J. They put up with T.J., even though she was a girl, because she didn't *act* much like a girl. Sometimes she was even almost fun to have around.

"Hey, James," said Norman, opening his milk carton. "Happy birthday! Did you get any good presents?"

James sighed again as he looked at his new red lunch box. "Nah, nothing special. But since it's my birthday, does anyone want to trade lunches—just once?"

Pete and Mike and Norman made gagging noises, and even T.J. shook her head.

"Sorry, James," she said, "but I've seen what your mom puts in your lunch box. I think I'll just stick with my bologna."

"Yeah," said James, gloomily. "That's what I thought."

He watched as T.J. took a big bite of her bologna sandwich. His mouth got drippy as Pete took a chocolate doughnut from his lunch. It sure beat bean sprouts.

Then James opened his lunch box.

"What—?" he gasped when he saw his lunch. "How—?" The other kids turned and stared, too.

The bean sprouts were gone. So were the dried apricots and the raw cauliflower and the liver on whole wheat. What James saw in his lunch box were hot dogs—two of them, with chili and cheese and onions—and a whole bag of cheese curls, and chocolate bars—one with nuts and one without.

"That's *your* lunch?" asked Norman. "Are you sure you've got the right lunch box?"

"This is weird," said Mike. "Maybe somebody stole your lunch and put theirs in your box."

T.J. snorted. "Are you kidding?" she said. "With the crummy lunches he brings? Who would do that?"

"Maybe your mom was just being nice because it's your birthday," Pete suggested.

"Yeah," said James. "That's got to be it." But hadn't he seen his mother dropping a bag of bean sprouts into his lunch box?

"Well," said T.J. with her mouth full of bologna. "I wouldn't waste the whole lunch hour worrying about it. Better enjoy it while you can."

12

"Yeah," said James, looking at the two hot dogs. "Hey, yeah!" and he crammed his mouth full of hot dog, chili, and bun.

In the bus on the way home, James decided his mother must have packed the delicious lunch. Maybe while he was getting his jacket out of the closet, she had switched the bean sprouts for hot dogs. How else could he explain it?

Tomorrow she would probably pack bean sprouts again. But for once, at least, everyone had wanted to trade lunches with him.

When James got home, his mother was in the kitchen, shredding zucchini and eggplant for a casserole.

"Uh—thanks for the great lunch, Mom," said James, putting his lunch box on the kitchen table.

His mother smiled.

"Why, you're welcome," she answered. "I thought your cauliflower looked very fresh and crisp. And I dried the apricots myself, last summer. James? James, why are you staring at me that way?"

If his mother didn't do it, then who did? James wondered.

James thought about it all through his healthy, nutritious birthday dinner. He wondered about it afterward, while he opened his presents and his mother and his aunt Bessie sang "Happy Birthday to You." He wondered about it while he put on his pajamas and brushed his teeth. And he wondered about it in bed, right up to the very minute he fell asleep.

# CHAPTER 3

# The Magic Lunch Box

The next morning, James watched closely as his mother packed him a lunch of rice cakes, hard-boiled eggs, spinach leaves— and bean sprouts. He even took the new lunch box with him while he went to the closet for his coat, so she wouldn't have a chance to switch lunches.

At school, he set his lunch box at the very front of the classroom shelves, where he could keep an eye on it all morning. He could have sworn no one had gone near his lunch box.

But at noon, when he opened it in the lunchroom, he saw—barbecued beef sandwiches! And crisp onion rings and big dill pickles and two big chocolate fudge brownies with walnuts on top!

Everyone's eyes bugged out.

"Wow!" said T.J., poking at a pickle. "What's gotten into your mom? She sick or something?"

James shook his head.

"It's not my mom," he said. "It wasn't her yesterday, either. I don't know who it is."

Carefully, he picked up one of the sandwiches and took a big bite.

"Hey!" he said with his mouth full. "This stuff is still warm!"

"How can it be?" Norman demanded. "It's been sitting on a shelf all morning!"

"I don't know!" James took an onion ring —still warm. "I just don't know! Unless—"

Suddenly a crazy idea popped into his head. Oh no! It couldn't be! Or could it?

"Quick," he said. "One of you give me something from your lunch!"

17

"Why should we?" asked Pete. "You've got a better lunch than any of us!"

"Don't argue!" James was already emptying his lunch box, setting the food out on the table. "I want to try something."

Mike shrugged. "Well," he said, "my mom gave me liverwurst today. I've never liked it much. I'll trade it for one of your brownies."

"You got it." James pushed the brownie across the table to Mike and took back half a liverwurst sandwich. "Now, let's see—"

"What are you doing?" Mike asked as James shoved the sandwich into his new lunch box, closing and latching the lid.

"You'll see," James told him. "Hmmm—I don't know how long this takes. Someone count to fifty—slowly."

T.J., Mike, Pete, and Norman exchanged funny looks, but then T.J. began counting. "One, two, three, four—"

"Slower," James interrupted, still staring at his lunch box.

"Five—six—seven . . ."

When T.J. counted "forty-eight—forty-

18

nine—fifty," James unlatched the lid of his lunch box.

"Okay, everybody," he said, "get ready for this. If it's what I think it is..."

He opened the red lunch box.

"What did you *do?*" gasped Norman, who was closest.

"What *is* it?" demanded Pete and Mike and T.J., all crowding in for a better look.

"It's not possible," said James, taking a triple-decker cheeseburger from his lunch box. "It's just not possible. But it happened!"

"What kind of trick are you playing on us, James?" T.J. said with her hands on her hips. "Did you really think we'd fall for that?"

James took a deep breath.

"Listen, everybody," he said. "I think I can explain..."

It took most of the lunch hour, while Mike ate the cheeseburger, for James to tell them about his Uncle Wesley and his adventures in faraway places and the note he had sent with the lunch box.

"So I think," he finished, "some kind of magic is going on. I mean, how else can you explain it?"

"Magic," said T.J. "I don't know if I believe in that—not *real* magic, anyway."

"All I know," said James, "is that when I put that sandwich into my lunch box, it was filled with liverwurst. And when I took it out, it was a *real* cheeseburger."

"Yeah," T.J. admitted. "Can't argue with that."

Her face was just a little red when she asked, "Uh, James, you got room in your lunch box for my egg salad sandwich?"

James grinned. "Sure," he said. And a few seconds later, T.J. was happily biting into a submarine sandwich with everything on it.

"Wow, neat!" chorused Norman and Pete, swapping their carrot sticks and raisins for french fries and chocolate chip cookies.

"Uh, oh," said T.J. suddenly, out of the corner of her mouth. "Better keep it down, guys. Mean Mitchell has his eye on us."

A chill ran down James's back as he sneaked a look at Mean Mitchell sitting two tables away. Sure enough, the class bully was staring at them, and James didn't much like the nasty glint in his beady little eyes.

"Yeah, let's cool it with the lunch box for now," he agreed. "This is one thing I definitely don't want Mean Mitchell to find out about."

James wouldn't put anything past Mean Mitchell. He was the kind of kid who would knock a first-grader down to take his milk money. No sir, he thought again, as he latched the lid of his lunch box. He didn't want any trouble with Mean Mitchell.

# CHAPTER 4

# This Is the Life

James should have known that he couldn't keep his lunch box a secret forever. For the next few days, he was easily the most popular boy in the whole fourth grade. Everyone wanted to sit with him at lunch, and the kids who couldn't find seats at his table always found an excuse to walk past it so that they could ask him to change their tuna fish or hard-boiled eggs or meat loaf sandwiches in his wonderful lunch box.

Even his mother noticed how popular he had become. Now, after school and on weekends, the yard was full of kids, playing baseball, throwing Frisbees for James's dog, Tag, and riding skateboards in the driveway. And usually they managed to do a lot of their playing in back of the garage, where James would use his lunch box to change after-school snacks of apples and granola bars into potato chips and cupcakes.

"Yes sir, Tag," James said one evening when everyone else had gone home and the two of them were sitting all alone on the porch steps. "Yes sir, this is the life."

He dropped a handful of bean sprouts into his lunch box and firmly closed the lid. A minute later, he took out a chocolate bar, broke off a piece for Tag, and bit off a huge piece for himself.

Tag, his mouth full of chocolate, tilted his head and looked at James out of his funny brown-and-white face. James could almost swear he had winked.

Of course, it wasn't long before Mean Mitchell showed up at James's lunch table, shoving a pickle-loaf sandwich into his face

without even a "please." James quickly dropped the sandwich into his lunch box, latched the lid, and after a few seconds took out a sloppy joe. He held his breath until Mean Mitchell looked it over, nodded, and went back to his table.

"That was close," said T.J., as Norman gave a low whistle. "If I were you, James, I'd keep my eye on that lunch box. If Mean Mitchell makes up his mind to take it, it's as good as gone."

"Don't worry," James told her, trying to sound braver than he felt. "This is one thing Mean Mitchell's not getting."

So naturally, his wonderful lunch box disappeared the next day.

"James," said his mother as he ate his breakfast, "where's your new lunch box, the one your Uncle Wesley sent you? Did you leave it at school yesterday?"

James choked on a spoonful of grapefruit.

"No, Mom," he spluttered. "I'm sure I brought it home."

And he *was* sure, because he had spent

almost an hour behind the garage after school changing snacks for some of the kids.

"Strange," said his mother. She opened the kitchen cabinet and pointed to the empty place where he usually kept his lunch box. "See? Not there. Well, I suppose we can put your lunch in the old lunch box for once. But please, James, check in the school lost-and-found today, just in case. I don't know what your Uncle Wesley would say if he thought you had lost his birthday present."

"Yes, Mom," James said miserably as he watched her fill his old lunch box with wheat germ and yogurt, raw cabbage wedges, dried prunes—and bean sprouts.

# CHAPTER 5

# The Missing Lunch Box

"You *what?*" T.J. gasped when they sat down at the table in the lunchroom. "You *what?*" echoed Pete and Mike and Norman.

"I lost my lunch box," James answered. "I don't know what could have happened to it. I had it last night—remember, Norman? Out behind the garage."

"Did you check there?" Norman suggested. "Maybe you forgot to take it in last night."

"First place I looked," James said gloomily. "Not a sign of it. Just a few cookies in the grass."

"Wait a minute," said T.J. "I don't like the sound of this. James, think hard. Are you sure that the garage is the very last place you saw it?"

James thought so hard his nose wrinkled up to his forehead. Where *had* he seen his lunch box last? Had he helped himself to a snack while he was doing his homework in his room? Had he had a few goodies while he was reading comics under the covers in bed? No, he had still been too stuffed from the pepperoni pizza he had enjoyed behind the garage. Which meant—which meant—

"I'm sure the last time I had it was out there behind the garage," James told T.J.

T.J. leaned across the table and spoke in a whisper.

"Look over there at Mean Mitchell," she said. "Look what he has for lunch."

James and Norman and Mike and Pete looked.

"Fried chicken," James said, puzzled. "So what?"

"Don't you see?" T.J. sounded impatient.

"James, you must have left your lunch box outside last night, and Mean Mitchell must have stolen it."

James almost choked on a bean sprout.

"Do you think so?" he gasped. "Gosh, T.J., do you really think that's what happened?"

Norman and Mike and Pete all groaned.

"It has to be," Norman said. "Nothing else makes sense. Since when does Mean Mitchell ever have fried chicken in his lunch? The lunches his mom makes are almost as yucky as the ones you get."

"Besides," Mike added, "you know how he is. And you know he knew about your lunch box."

Pete was shaking his head back and forth. "Oh yeah," he agreed. "T.J. has to be right. Mean Mitchell's got your lunch box. You can count on it."

"You know what I bet?" said T.J. "I bet he changed his lunch before he got to school, then put it in his own lunch box so you wouldn't suspect anything."

"Yeah, that makes sense," James nodded.

"So now that we've figured that out, what are we going to do about it? I sure don't want to have to fight Mean Mitchell for my lunch box."

"He'd turn you into dog food," said T.J. "And don't look at me that way, James—it's the truth, and you know it. No, what we've got to do is make a plan."

"A plan?" asked Norman. "What kind of plan?"

"Well," said T.J., swallowing a sticky mouthful of peanut butter, "last week I watched a TV show that was all about this great detective, see? And whenever he had a case to solve, the first thing he did was to study the scene of the crime."

"The scene of the crime?" James asked. "You mean, behind my garage?"

T.J. nodded.

"Right after school, we all have to get together at your house," she said. "Maybe we can find some clue to help us figure out what Mean Mitchell has done with your lunch box."

"I can make it," said Norman.

"Me too," said Mike and Pete.

James just nodded, because his mouth was full of yogurt and wheat germ.

# CHAPTER 6

# Mean Mitchell, Lunch-Box Thief

After school that day, everyone rushed to James's backyard.

"Where's Tag?" T.J. asked as soon as she arrived.

"I don't know," said James. "I whistled for him, but he didn't come. I guess he's off chasing rabbits in the woods or something."

"Darn," said T.J. "I thought we could use him to help us track down your lunch box —you know, like a bloodhound or whatever those dogs are."

"I don't know," said James doubtfully.

"Tag is part beagle and part fox terrier. I don't think he'd make a very good blood-hound."

"Well, I guess we'll just have to manage without him," said T.J. with a sigh. "Come on, let's get a move on."

James led them all to the back of the garage.

"There's where I had my lunch box last night," he said, pointing. "Right there on that old tree stump."

"What do we do next?" asked Norman, shuffling his feet back and forth. "I didn't see that detective show."

"Now we've got to look for clues," T.J. explained. "You know, things like footprints or broken twigs—anything that might tell us where Mean Mitchell went with James's lunch box."

So they all got down on their hands and knees, each one facing a different direction, to look for anything that might be a clue. At first, there was nothing, no footprints, no broken twigs, but then—

"Is this a clue?" Mike asked. He pointed to something in the grass.

They all crowded around him to look.

"Oh, that," said James. "That's just a few old cookies. I told you about those, remember?"

"But it's our very first clue!" exclaimed T.J. triumphantly.

"It is?" asked Pete.

"Of course!" T.J. laughed. "Don't you get it? Those cookies were probably spilled out of James's lunch box!"

Then they all got it!

"Wow!" said James. "You mean—?"

"I mean," said T.J., "if Mean Mitchell didn't fasten the lid very tight, he might have left a whole trail of food behind him! All we've got to do is follow the trail to wherever he hid your lunch box!"

"And I see the next clue already!" yelled Pete, pointing. "You see, right across the alley there? A whole bunch more cookies!"

"After him!" yelled Norman, and they set off on the trail of Mean Mitchell, the lunch-box thief.

36

# CHAPTER 7

# The Old Hathaway House

This seems too easy, James thought. The trail of cookies led across Mrs. Murphy's backyard, under the Flanagans' clothesline, and through the Abernathy's hedge. Then it came to an end, and everybody looked around, confused for a minute or two.

Suddenly T.J.'s sharp eyes caught something half a block down the sidewalk.

"A cookie!" she cried when they had reached it. "What a pig that Mean Mitchell is! How many of those things can he eat?"

They quickly became very good at spotting clues. A cookie here, a cookie there— before they knew it, they were blocks away from James's house, almost all the way downtown.

"Listen!" said Mike. "What's that music?"

"Oh, no!" cried James, slapping his forehead with the back of his hand. "We forgot that the big high school football parade goes down Main Street this afternoon!"

"The trail is heading right for Main Street!" T.J. moaned. "If we don't find those clues before the parade gets there, there'll be nothing left! Come on! We have to hurry!"

Running fast, they pushed their way through the thick crowd lining up on Main Street to see the parade. The first marching band was only half a block away, trumpets blaring, drums rattling, tasseled boots strutting high and ready to squash a cookie to mush! Frantically, James looked this way and that, up and down Main Street. Where was the next clue?

T.J. spotted it first.

"Look!" she yelled. "Across the street, over there by the storm drain!"

It was another cookie.

"Hey, you kids!" yelled a traffic cop as they darted into the street. "You can't cross the street now. There's a parade coming! Hey!"

But they kept on going, right under the nose of the drum major in his tall hat, so close to the marching band that James felt a blast of air from the big tuba.

The trail led them on, down the crowded sidewalk, around the corner, and away from Main Street—a cookie here, a cookie there.

On Elm Street, where the road was being repaired, they were barely in time to save their next clue from being flattened by a big steamroller. At Sixth and Broadway, they were chased by a big dog as they followed the trail, and they had to scramble over a fence to get away from him. Back across Main Street—down Washington Avenue— up Maple Boulevard.

"James," said T.J., "do you realize what's

happening? We're headed back toward your house! Boy, that Mean Mitchell is even sneakier than I thought!"

"Yeah!" said James. "He never thought I'd think to look in my own neighborhood!"

"I don't like this, James," said Norman a few minutes later, as they followed bits of cookie across Maple and onto Pine. "Look where we're headed now!"

"What do you mean?" asked James, looking up for the first time in several minutes. "I don't know what—"

Then he stopped, feeling like someone had punched him in the stomach. They were standing in front of the old Hathaway house.

"Oh no!" he groaned. "We can't go in there!"

Every kid in town knew the old Hathaway house was haunted. No one had lived there in years, but people said that sometimes, late at night, you could hear screams and moans and could see a mysterious blue light shining from the tower window. That was where the *murder* had been. James wasn't sure what murder; he only knew the house was big and gray and spooky-looking, and he wouldn't go inside it for a million dollars.

And the trail of cookies led right up the sidewalk to the rickety front porch!

"We've got to go in there," said T.J. "How else are we going to find your lunch box? Besides, those are just old stories, anyway. I think."

"I don't know, T.J.," Pete said, shaking his head. "My big brother says awful things have happened to people there. We could disappear and never be heard from again!"

"Besides," said Mike, "it's going to be dark pretty soon. I definitely don't want to be here after dark!"

"They might be right, T.J.," James agreed. "It's too dangerous. It might not be worth it."

T.J. looked disgusted.

"Okay," she said, throwing her hands up into the air. "You don't want to go, we don't go. If you're sure you don't mind eating

bean sprouts for the rest of your life."

James thought about all those bean sprouts. Then he took a big breath, pushed the old gate open with a terrible squeak, and stepped through.

"All right, all right," he said. "I'm going after my lunch box."

With a smile, T.J. followed him. Norman and Mike and Pete looked at each other. Then, shrugging their shoulders, they followed too.

# CHAPTER 8

# He's Got a Lot of Nerve!

Outside there was afternoon sunlight on Pine Street, but the minute James and the other kids stepped into the Hathaway yard, it was dark. Partly it was because the yard was so full of trees—tall, gloomy old pines and elms and cedars that grew so close together they hardly let any light through. But partly it was because the house was so big that it blocked the sky. It was like a huge animal crouched at the end of the sidewalk, waiting to pounce on them the second they got close enough. The boys kept turning and looking over their shoulders, tiptoeing as quietly as if there really were someone in the old house to hear them. Even T.J. had gotten very quiet as they followed the trail of cookies up the long, long sidewalk. The only sounds were the moaning of the wind in the trees and the squeaking branches and the pounding of their own hearts.

James was in the lead, so he was the first one up the sagging wooden steps and onto the front porch. Each stair groaned as he tiptoed up it, trying to step around the places where the wood was almost rotted through. Up on the porch it was darker than ever and colder too, with the last of the sunshine shut out by the roof. The trail of cookies led across the porch.

"This porch is half-rotten," said James, pointing to a big hole. "Maybe we should—"

Crash! It sounded as if the sky had fallen on the porch roof! They jumped as if they had been shot, and before their feet even had time to touch ground again, they were off the porch, around the corner, and away from the old house, stopping to catch their breath only when they were halfway to the street.

"Look," said T.J., pointing. "It was just an old dead branch. See? It landed on the roof of the porch."

Sure enough, a huge branch lay across the roof, its end sticking through a broken window. The kids smiled at each other, feeling foolish.

"I don't care," said James. "One time on that porch was enough for me. I'm not going back up there, not even if I have to eat bean sprouts for the rest of my life."

"It's okay," said T.J. "We don't have to. Look!"

She pointed to the trail of cookies leading through a gap in the fence and back out to the street.

"That's lucky for you, James!" said Norman. "Because I wasn't going back to that house for anything!"

They were in such a hurry to get out of

the Hathaway yard, they squeezed through the broken fence in one big clump.

"Now where?" asked Pete when they were standing in the bright sunshine.

"There!" Mike spotted a cookie in the middle of the street, and they were off again.

"We're definitely headed back toward your house, James," T.J. said. "What do you think that sneaky Mean Mitchell could have been up to?"

"I saw that on a detective show," James remembered. "Sometimes a crook hides his loot right out in plain sight, and that's the very place where no one would ever think to look for it! Mean Mitchell thinks we'd never suspect him of hiding my lunch box practically in my own backyard! I just hope—oh no!"

He skidded to a stop and moaned.

"What is it, James?" Norman asked.

James sighed. "I was just going to say that I hope Mean Mitchell didn't cut through that old vacant lot—you know, the

48

one with all the weeds and tin cans and blackberry bushes? But..."

Then they saw it too—a big chocolate chip cookie, caught like a strange berry right in the middle of a tangle of blackberry bushes.

"'Oh no' is right," said Norman. "My mom made me pick blackberries in there last summer so she could make jelly. Some of those thorns are a foot long!"

Even T.J. was beginning to look a little discouraged.

"Well, come on," she said. "We can't give up now, not after the Hathaway house. Besides, it's for a good cause, remember?"

"Ow!" yelped James as a blackberry branch grabbed him around the ankles.

"Ow! Ow! Ow! Ow!" echoed Norman and Pete and Mike and T.J. as the wicked thorns slashed at their necks and their hands and their faces.

But there was a cookie, and over by an old tire was another one, and finally, at the very edge of the vacant lot, one more.

"Hooray!" yelled T.J. as they finally broke free of the last blackberry bush. "We're out!"

"And there's your next clue!" said Mike, pointing. "And you're right, T.J.—the trail's leading us straight back to James's house!"

They ran the last block, hot on a trail of cookies.

"Why, he did—he came back to my house!" James said. "He's got a lot of nerve!"

"Not only that, it looks like he's taken the lunch box right back where it came from— behind your garage," T.J. pointed out as they followed the trail. "What is he up to?"

"Listen!" said Pete suddenly. "There's somebody behind the garage right now!"

They froze in their tracks, careful not to make a sound. Sure enough, there was a strange noise coming from behind the garage—a little thump as if somebody were dropping something, then a click as if somebody had just closed a lunch-box lid, then a chewing, gulping, lip-smacking sound as if somebody were wolfing down something delicious.

"My lunch box!" said James. He sounded angry. "And he's using it in my very own yard!"

"Mean Mitchell?" Norman's voice came out in a funny squeak. "*Here? Now?*"

"I'm going to get my lunch box back!" James began to march toward the garage. He was so mad, he forgot to be scared.

"Wait for us, James," said T.J., glaring at the boys. "We're coming with you!"

# CHAPTER 9

# The Thief Is Discovered

Their sneakers made no sound in the grass as they moved toward the garage and the thumping-clicking-chewing sounds.

Carefully, James flattened himself against the side of the garage and shuffled sideways toward the back. Carefully, the others followed him.

"Shh!" James whispered, with his finger on his lips. "When I say 'now,' we all jump out and grab him!"

He took a deep breath, clenched his hands into fists, and gathered up all of his courage. Then slowly, very slowly, he poked his head around the corner of the garage...

"What!" the others all heard him gasp. "I don't believe it! I just don't believe it!"

And then he began to laugh.

"What on earth—?" said T.J., and then they all went scrambling around the corner of the garage to see what Mean Mitchell could possibly be doing to make James laugh like that.

What they saw made them stop as if they had hit an invisible wall. The boys just stood there with their mouths hanging open, but T.J. sat down with a thud.

"Don't tell me!" she groaned. "You mean *this* is our lunch-box thief?"

Tag looked up at them proudly from his funny brown-and-white face. Then he took another piece of dry dog food from his food dish, dropped it into the lunch box— *thump*, nosed the lid shut—*click*, and nosed it open again. Then—chew, gulp, smack—a chocolate chip cookie disappeared almost before they had time to see what it was.

"That's our lunch-box thief," said James. "He must have been carrying that thing around, spilling cookies everywhere he went, all day."

For a minute, remembering the traffic cop and the Hathaway house and the blackberry patch, they just stared at each other. Then T.J. began to laugh too, then Norman, then Pete and Mike.

"I can't believe it," T.J. spluttered. "We followed a *dog* around all afternoon!"

"Woof!" Tag agreed politely with his mouth full of cookie crumbs.

At that, everybody rolled on the ground and laughed some more. Tag tilted his head and stared at them with a puzzled expression on his face.

Suddenly, James heard the back door bang.

"James!" called his mother from the porch. "Oh, there you are! Where in the world have you been? I've been calling you!"

James and his friends looked at each

other, still trying to stop laughing.

"Uh—just around, Mom," he said at last. "Big parade on Main Street today."

"Oh, that's nice," his mother said. "But next time ask, okay? You'd better come in now. Time to get washed for dinner. Oh, and your friends can stay, too, if they want —there's plenty of soybean meat loaf."

She went back into the house.

"Uh—thanks, but no thanks," said T.J. quickly. "I've got homework."

"Me too," echoed Norman and Mike and Pete.

James grinned. "That's okay," he said. "I wouldn't eat the stuff if I didn't have to. But remember, tomorrow at lunch—" He picked up his lunch box and tapped it.

"Yeah!" they said. "Yeah!" And waving good-bye, they went through the gate.

"Coming, Mom!" James yelled, running across the backyard with Tag at his heels. "And Mom—guess what? I found my lunch box!"